EDGAR ALLAN POE

THE MURDERS IN THE RUE MORGUE
and
THE GOLD BUG

Edited by Solveig Odland
Illustrations by Oskar Jørgensen

The vocabulary is based on
Michael West: A General Service List of
English Words, revised & enlarged edition, 1953
Birger Thorén: 10.000 Words for 10 Years of English, 1990
J.A. van Ek: The Threshold Level,
Council of Europe Press, 1990
The British National Corpus, Oxford, 1996

Series editors:
Ulla Malmmose and Charlotte Bistrup

Cover layout: Mette Plesner
Cover illustration: Jeannine Petty/County Studio

Copyright © 1989 EASY READERS, Copenhagen
- a subsidiary of Lindhardt og Ringhof Forlag A/S,
an Egmont company.
ISBN Denmark 978-87-23-90117-0
www.easyreader.dk
The CEFR levels stated on the back of the book
are approximate levels.

Easy Readers
EGMONT

Printed in Denmark by
Sangill Grafisk Produktion, Holme-Olstrup

EDGAR ALLAN POE

was born in Boston, USA in 1809 of an English mother and an Irish American father, both itinerant actors. They died before Edgar was three years old and the child was taken into the home of a Richmond merchant, John Allan.

Poe studied at the University of Virginia, but his relationship with his foster-father was not good and he was forced to withdraw from university because Allan refused to finance him. In 1830 he entered West Point Military Academy, but was dismissed for not obeying orders.

He became editor of various magazines, which published some of his best stories: "Tales of the Grotesque and Arabesque", 1839, "The Murders in the Rue Morgue", 1841, and "The Gold Bug", 1843.

He achieved respect as a literary critic but it was not until the publication of "The Raven and Other Poems" in 1845 that he gained success as a writer. The poems "Annabel Lee", written in memory of his wife who died very young, and "The Bells", both 1849, made him widely popular.

Poe published several tales and horror stories, among which the most remarkable are "The Fall of the House of Usher", 1839, which ranks undoubtedly among the short-fiction masterpieces of all time, "The Mystery of Marie Roget«, 1842, and "The Cask of Amontillado", 1846.

There can be little doubt that Poe was a disturbed and tormented man, and like so many of his characters, often driven to the brink of madness. He died in 1849, a few years after his wife, in the same grim poverty which characterized most of his life.

Poe was translated into French by Baudelaire and Mallarmé and had a profound influence on the Symbolist school. Outside France his influence has also been considerable. Robert Louis Stevenson and Arthur Conan Doyle both acknowledge their debts to Poe's work.

From his tales we trace the growth of the detective story. Here we see Poe's passion for the intellectual with its coldly analytical approach to solving the problems – far from all romanticism. Aguste Dupin exhibits his extraordinary abilities for deduction and analysis in "The Murders in the Rue Morgue" and "The Mystery of Marie Roget", thus becoming the model for many other famous private investigators such as Sherlock Holmes, Hercule Poirot and Lord Peter Wimsey.

CONTENTS
The Murders in the Rue Morgue 5
The Gold Bug 46

The Murders in the Rue Morgue

Residing in Paris during the spring and part of the summer of 18 –, I became familiar with a Monsieur C. Auguste Dupin. This gentleman was of an excellent – indeed of a distinguished family. By a variety of sad events, however, he had become so poor that the strength of his character suffered from it. He stopped taking any interest in the world, not caring even to try to get his fortune back. A small part of his *patrimony* was still in his possession and from the income of this, he managed to get the necessaries of life. Books were his only luxury.

Our first meeting was in a small library in the *Rue* Montmartre, where by accident we were both looking for the same rare book. We saw each other again and again. I was deeply interested in the little family history which he detailed to me as *candidly* as only a Frenchman can do when the talk is about himself.

I was astonished, too, at the huge amount of books he had read; and, above all, my soul was set on fire by his fresh and lively imagination. I felt that while I was in Paris, the company of such a man would be to me a treasure beyond prize, and I told him so, quite openly.

It was at length arranged that we should live together during my stay in the city. As my state of affairs was less troubled than his own, I was permitted to be

---

reside, to have one's home
patrimony, property passed on to a person by parents or other members of the family
Rue, (French) street
candidly, openly, without hiding anything

at the expense of the *mansion* we rented in a retired part of the Fauburg St. Germain. It was an old, time-eaten house which had long been deserted for reasons into which we did not inquire. This extraordinary building we furnished in a style which suited the rather fantastic *gloom* of our common temper.

Had our way of life at this place been known to the world, we should have been regarded as madmen, although of a harmless nature. We lived alone and admitted no visitors. Indeed, our address had been carefully kept a secret from anybody who knew me; and it had been many years since Dupin had been known in Paris. We existed within ourselves alone.

My friend enjoyed the hours of the night, he was attracted by the dark. I, quietly, fell into this *bizarrerie*, as into all his others, giving myself up to his wild fan-

---

mansion, large house
gloom, dark state of mind
bizarrerie, (French) unusual liking or behaviour

cies. At the early morning light we closed all the heavy *shutters* of our old building and lighted a couple of *candles*. By the weak rays of these we then busied our souls in dreams reading, writing, or talking until the true Darkness arrived. Then we went out into the streets, walking along arm-in-arm, continuing the subject of our discussion. We went far and wide until a late hour, seeking amongst the lights and shadows of the crowded city, all the excitement of the mind which quiet observation can afford.

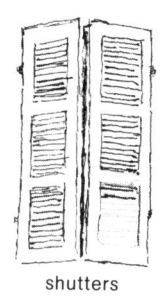

shutters

candle

At such times I could not help remarking and admiring a peculiar *analytical* ability in Dupin. He clearly took delight in its exercise and boasted to me that he often could see through the minds of other men as seeing through a window.

As the strong man takes delight in such exercises as call his muscles into action, so the *analyst* enjoys even the most *trivial* occupation of the mind in which he

---

analytical, that solves a problem by using reason and logic, and by taking into consideration all the details that the problem may consist of
analyst, person with an analytical mind
trivial, of little importance

must *analyse* and reason. The analyst not only observes carefully, in silence, and has an excellent memory. He also has the necessary knowledge of what to observe. What is important is the quality of the observation.

Often, when we were *strolling* down the streets in silence, at night, Dupin would surprise me with his skill. He sometimes would say out loud what was on my mind, finishing my chain of thoughts. He had noticed what had caught my attention while walking down the street; when I had looked up at a person passing us, and other such trivial details. All these added up made him able to read my mind.

One evening, as we were out on our usual walk, we were looking over an evening *edition* of the 'Gazette des Tribuneaux'*, when the following words caught our attention:

"EXTRAORDINARY MURDERS. This morning, about three o clock, the *inhabitants* of the Quartier St Roch were awoken by a number of terrible screams coming from the fourth story of a house in the Rue Morgue. The only persons living in this house were *Madame* L'Espanaye, and her daughter, *Mademoiselle* Camille L'Espanaye.

"The gate was locked, which caused some delay. It was finally broken and eight or ten of the neighbours

---

analyse, to examine carefully
stroll, to walk without hurry
edition, a number of copies (of a newspaper or book) printed at the same time
*a newspaper
inhabitant, person who lives permanently in a place
Madame, Mademoiselle, (French) Mrs, Miss

entered the gateway together with 2 *gendarmes*. By this time the cries had stopped, but as the party entered the house and rushed up the first flight of stairs, two or more rough voices were distinguished. They seemed to come from the upper part of the house. As the second landing was reached, these sounds, also, had stopped, and everything remained perfectly quiet. The party spread themselves and hurried from room to room. Upon arriving at a large *chamber* at the back of the fourth story, a sight presented itself which struck everyone with *horror*. The door of the room had been found locked, with the key inside, and had been forced open.

---

gendarme, (French) policeman
chamber, room
horror, great fear and dislike

"The *apartment* was in the wildest disorder, the furniture broken and thrown about in all directions. There was only one *bedstead*; and from this the bed had been removed, and thrown into the middle of the floor. On a chair lay a *razor* with blood all over it. On the floor of the fire-place were some grey *tresses* of human hair, also with blood on them, and seeming to have been pulled out by the roots. On the floor were found two bags, containing nearly four thousand *francs* in gold. There was a *chest of drawers* in one corner. The drawers were open and had, it seemed, been searched. A small iron box was discovered near the bed. It was open, with the key still in the door. It had no contents beyond a few old letters, and other papers

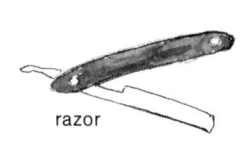

---

apartment, (American) flat
bedstead, frame of a bed
razor, sharp instrument used for shaving hair from the skin
franc, French coin

of little importance.

"Madame L'Espanaye had disappeared. But as an unusual quantity of *soot* was observed in the fire-place, a search was made in the chimney, and (horrible to tell!) the *corpse* of the daughter, head downward, was dragged therefrom. It had been forced up the narrow chimney. The body was quite warm. The skin was torn, no doubt because of the violence with which the body had been forced up the chimney and pulled out again. Upon the throat were dark *bruises* and deep marks of finger nails as if she had been *strangled* to death.

"After a careful examination of every part of the house, without further discovery, the party made its way into a small yard at the back of the building. Here lay the corpse of the old lady, with her throat so entirely cut that, upon an attempt to raise her, the head fell off. The body, as well as the head, was terribly *mutilated* the former so much that it scarcely looked human.

"To this horrible mystery there is not as yet, we believe, the slightest *clue*."

In the next day's paper these particulars were added:

"THE TRAGEDY OF THE RUE MORGUE. A large number of persons has been examined in relation to this most extraordinary and frightful affair, but

---

soot, the black powder left in chimneys after a fire
corpse, a dead body
bruise, mark on the skin caused by a blow or pressure
strangle, to kill by holding tight around a person's neck
mutilate, to cut off a limb or damage badly
clue, a fact forming a key to the solution of a problem

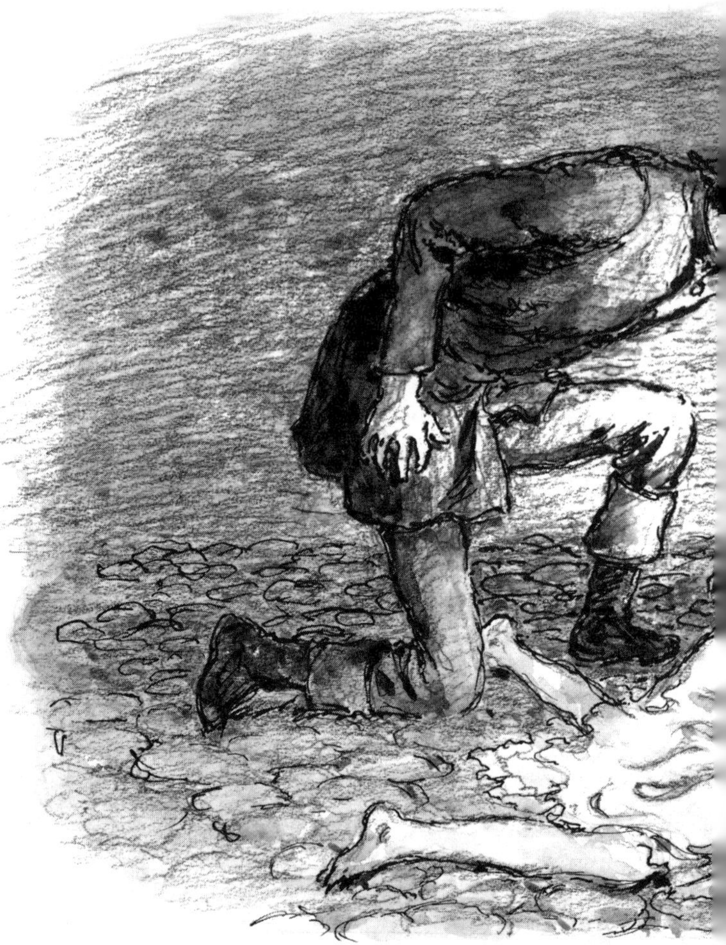

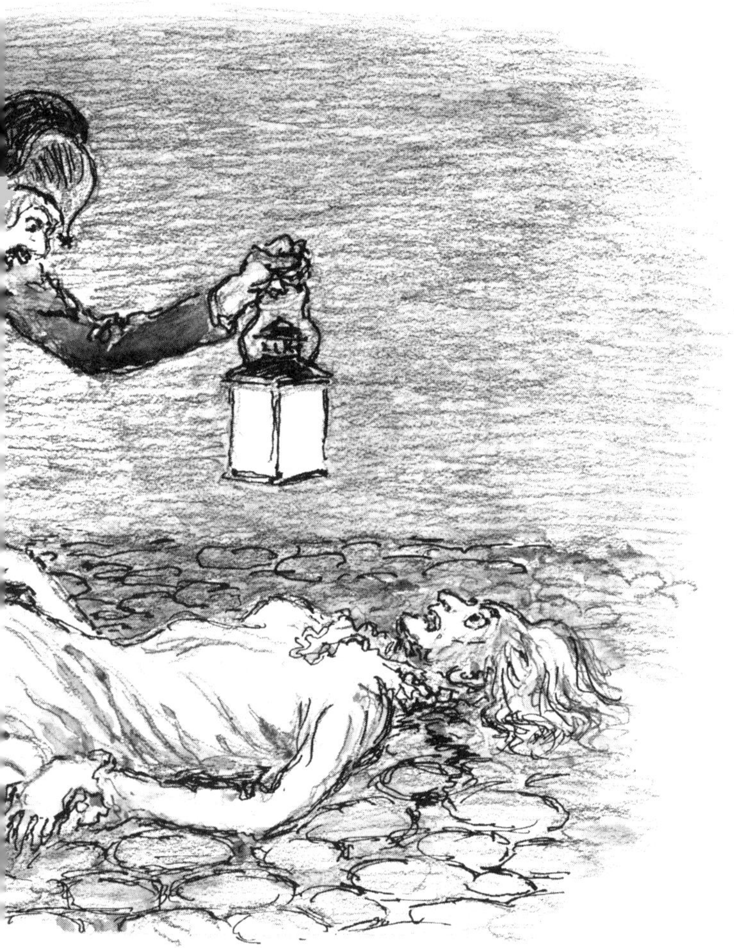

nothing whatever has been found to throw light upon it. We give below the declarations of the witnesses:

"Pauline Dubourg, *laundress, deposes* that she has known both the *deceased* for three years, having washed for them during that period. The old lady and her daughter seemed on good terms. They were excellent pay. Could not speak in regard to their way or means of living. Believed that Madame L. told fortunes for a living. Was known to have money *put by*. Never met any persons in the house when she called for the clothes or took them home. Was sure they had no servant in employ. There appeared to be no furniture in any part of the building except in the fourth story.

"Pierre Moreau, *tobacconist*, deposes that he has been in the habit of selling small quantities of tobacco and *snuff* to Madame L'Epanaye for nearly four years. Was born in the neighbourhood, and has always resided there. The deceased and her daughter had occupied the house in which the corpses were found, for more than six years. The house was the property of Madame L. She did not let any part of the house. The old lady was childish. Witness had seen the daughter some five or six times during the six years. The two lived an extremely retired life, were known to have money. Had heard it said among the neighbours that Madame L. told fortunes – did not believe it. Had not

---

laundress, a woman who washes and irons clothes
depose, to tell (the police) as a witness
the deceased, dead person(s)
put by, to save (money)
tobacconist, a person who sells tobacco, cigarettes etc.
snuff, powdered tobacco for sniffing up the nose

seen any person enter the door except the old lady and the daughter, a porter once or twice, and a *physician* some eight or ten times.

"Many other persons, neighbours, gave *evidence* to the same effect. No visitors had ever been seen. It was not known whether there were any living relatives of Madame L. or her daughter. The shutters of the front windows were seldom opened. Those at the back of the house were always closed, with the exception of the large back room, fourth story. The house was a good house – not very old.

"Isidore Muset, gendarme, deposes that he was called to the house about three o'clock in the morning, and found some twenty or thirty persons at the gateway, trying to get in. He forced the gate open at which time the screams suddenly stopped. They seemed to be screams of some person (or persons) in great *agony* – were long and drawn out, not short and quick. Witness led the way upstairs. Upon reaching the first landing, heard two loud voices arguing angrily, the one a *gruff* voice, the other much *shriller*, a very strange voice. Could distinguish some words of the former, which was that of a Frenchman. Was certain that it was not a woman's voice. The shrill voice was that of a foreigner. Could not be sure whether it was the voice of a man or a woman. Could not make out what was said, but believed the language to be Spanish. The state of the room and of the bodies was

---

physician, doctor of medicine
evidence, here, information given to the police
agony, great pain or suffering
gruff, rough and unfriendly
shrill, sharp

described by this witness as we described them yesterday.

"Henry Duval, a neighbour, and by trade a *silversmith*, deposes that he was one of the party who first entered the house. Confirms the evidence already given by Muset in general. As soon as they forced an entrance, they *re*closed the door, to keep out the crowd, which collected fast, even though it was very late. The shrill voice, the witness thinks, was that of an Italian. Was certain it was not French. Was not *acquainted with* the Italian language. Could not be sure that it was a man's voice. It might have been a woman's. Could not distinguish the words. Knew Madame L. and her daughter. Had talked with both of them frequently. Was sure that the shrill voice was not that of either of the deceased.

"M. Odenheimer, *restaurateur*. This witness is a native of Amsterdam and does not speak French. Was passing the house at the time of the screams. They lasted for several minutes, probably ten. They were long and loud – awful to listen to. Was one of those who entered the building. Supported the *previous* evidence in every respect but one. Was sure that the shrill voice was of a man – of a Frenchman. Could not distinguish the words. They were loud and quick unequal spoken, it seemed, in fear as well as in anger. The voice was *harsh* – not so much shrill as harsh. The deep voice

---

silversmith, a person who makes or sells silver articles
re-, again
acquainted with, to be familiar with; to know
restaurateur, the owner or manager of a restaurant
previous, earlier
harsh, rough

said 'mon Dieu'* several times.

"Jules Mignaud, banker, of the firm of Mignaud and Sons, Rue Deloraine. Is the elder Mignaud. Madame L'Espanaye had some property. Had opened an account with his banking house eight years earlier. Made frequent *deposits* in small sums. Three days before her death she took out in person the sum of 4,000 francs. This sum was paid in gold, and a clerk sent home with the money.

"Adolphe Le Bon, clerk to Mignaud and Sons, deposes that on the day in question, about noon, he accompanied Madame L'Espanaye to her home with the 4,000 francs, put up in two bags. Mademoiselle L. opened the door and took from his hands one of the bags, while the old lady relieved him of the other. He then bowed and left. Did not see any person in the street at the time. It is a small, lonely street.

"William Bird, tailor, deposes that he was one of the party who entered the house. Is an Englishman. Has lived in Paris two years. Was one of the first to go up the stairs. Heard the voices arguing. The gruff voice was that of a Frenchman. Could clearly hear 'mon Dieu.' There was a sound at the moment as of several persons struggling. The shrill voice was very loud – louder than the gruff one. Is sure that it was not the voice of an Englishman. Appeared to be that of a German. Might have been a woman's voice. Does not understand German.

"Four of the above named witnesses, being recalled, deposed that the door of the chamber in which was

---

*French, my God
deposit, here, the money put into a bank

found the body of Mademoiselle L. was locked on the inside when the party reached it. Everything was perfectly silent – no noises of any kind. Upon forcing the door no person was seen. The windows, both of the back and front room, were shut and firmly fastened from within. A door between the two rooms was closed, but not locked. The door leading from the front room into the passage was locked, with the key on the inside. A small room in the front of the house, on the fourth story, at the head of the passage, was open. This room was crowded with old beds, boxes and so forth. These were carefully removed and searched. There was not an inch of any part of the house which was not carefully searched. Sweeping-brushes were sent up and down the chimneys. The time passing between the hearing of the voices and the breaking open of the room door was stated by the witnesses to have been three to five minutes. The door was opened with difficulty.

"Alfonzo Garcia, *undertaker*, deposes that he resides in the Rue Morgue. Is a native of Spain. Was one of the party who entered the house. Did not go upstairs. Is a very nervous man. Heard the voices arguing. The gruff voice was that of a Frenchman. Could not distinguish what was said. The shrill voice was that of an Englishman, is sure of that. Does not understand English.

"Several witnesses, recalled, here testified that the chimneys of all the rooms on the fourth story were too narrow to admit the passage of a human being. There

---

undertaker, one who makes the necessary arrangements when a person is dead

is no back passage by which any one could have descended while the party went upstairs. The body of Mademoiselle L'Espanaye was so firmly pressed into the chimney that it could not be got down until four or five of the party united their strength.

"Paul Dumas, physician, deposes that he was called to view the bodies about day-break. They were both then lying in the chamber where Mademoiselle L. was found. The corpse of the young lady was much bruised and the skin was torn. The fact that it had been forced up the chimney would account for these appearances. There were several deep *scratches* on her throat just below the chin, together with a series of *livid* spots, marks of fingers, it seemed. Her eye-balls were sticking out and the tongue had been bitten through. In the opinion of M. Dumas, Mademoiselle L'Espanaye had been strangled to death by some person or persons unknown. The corpse of the mother was horribly mutilated. All the bones of the right leg and arm were more or less *shattered*. The whole body was dreadfully bruised. A heavy club of wood, or a broad bar of iron – a chair – any large, heavy weapon would have produced such results in the hands of a very powerful man. No woman could have given such blows with any instrument. The head of the deceased, when seen by witness, was entirely separated from the body, and was also greatly shattered. The throat had been cut with some very sharp instrument – probably with a razor.

---

scratch, a line – here in the surface of the skin – caused by a sharp instrument
livid, the bluish colour of a bruise
shatter, to break in small pieces, suddenly or forcefully

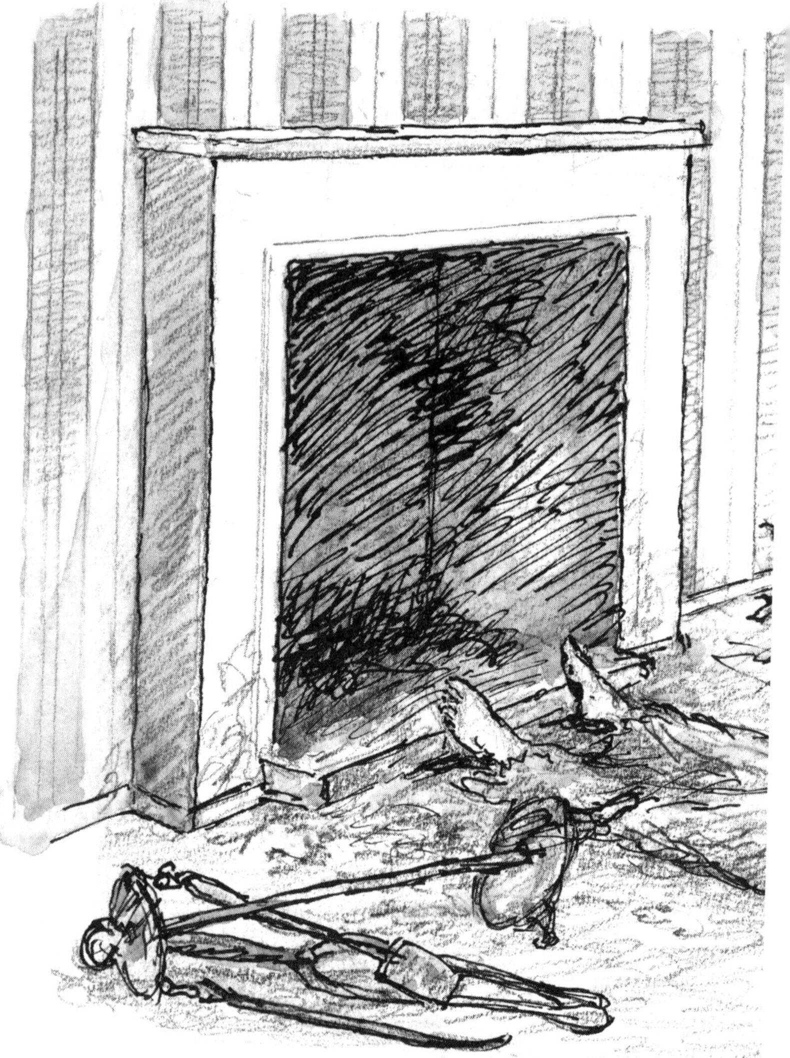

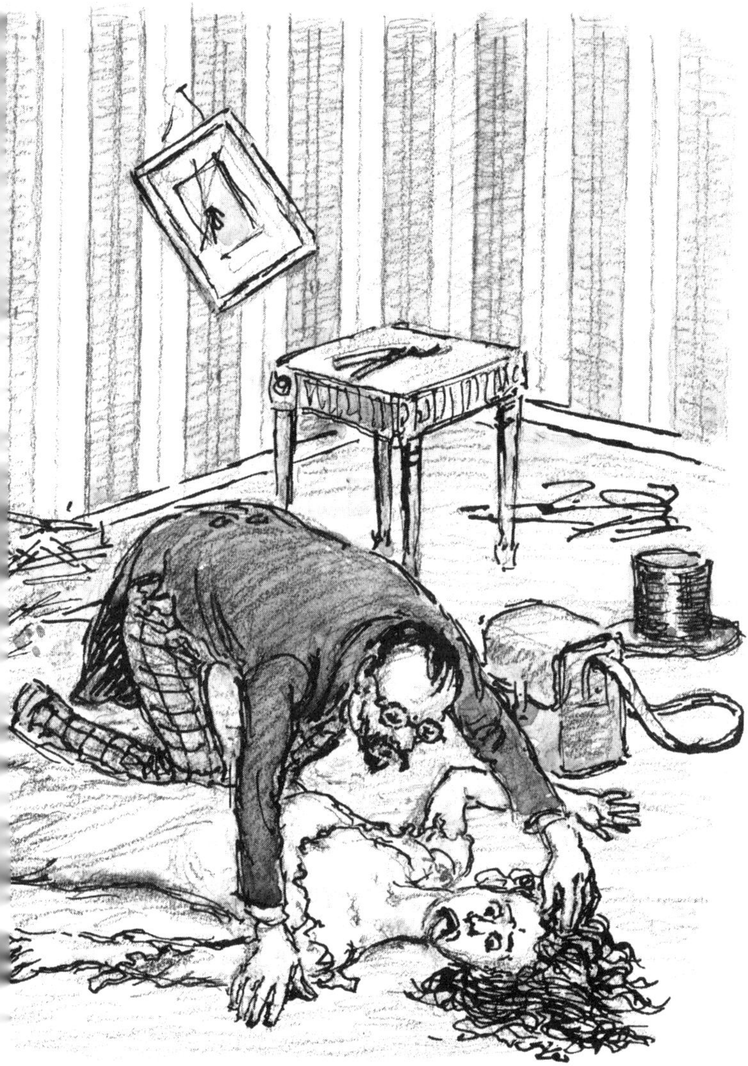

"Nothing farther of importance was brought forward, although several other persons were examined. A murder so mysterious in all its particulars was never before *committed* in Paris if indeed a murder had been committed at all. The police was entirely at a loss, which is unusual in affairs of this nature. There is not, however, the shadow of a clue to be found."

The evening edition of the paper stated that the greatest excitement still continued in the Quartier St Roch – that the place in question had been carefully researched, witnesses had been examined once more, all to no purpose. Adolphe Le Bon had been arrested, however, and *imprisoned* – although nothing appeared to indicate that he had anything to do with the crime beyond the facts already stated in detail.

Dupin seemed strangely interested in the progress of this affair – at least so I judged from his manner, for he made no comments. It was only after the information that Le Bon had been imprisoned, that he asked me my opinion about the murders.

I could only agree with all Paris in considering them an *insoluble* mystery. I saw no means by which it would be possible to find the murderer.

"We must not judge of the means," said Dupin, "by this shell of an examination. The Parisian police, so highly praised for being sharp and quick, are clever, but there is no *method* in their work, beyond the method of the moment.

Their results are often surprising, but for the most

---

commit, to carry out (a crime)
imprison, to put to prison
insoluble, that cannot be solved
method, a regular, definite way of doing something

part they are brought about by simple hard work and activity. When these qualities are useless, their plans fail. Vidocq, for example, was a good guesser and a hard-working man. But, without educated thought, he often made mistakes because he was too eager and hard-working. He could not see clearly as he was holding the object too close. He might see, perhaps, one or two points with unusual clearness, but in doing so he, necessarily, lost sight of the matter as a whole.

"As for these murders, let us enter into some examinations for ourselves, before we make up an opinion about them. An inquiry will be amusing to us," (I thought this an odd term, so applied, but said nothing), "and, besides, Le Bon once did me a service, and that I have not forgotten. We will go and see the *premises* with our own eyes. I know G –, the Chief of Police, and shall have no difficulty in getting the necessary permission."

We got the permission and continued at once to the Rue Morgue. This is one of the small streets which run between the Rue Richilieu and the Rue St Roch. It was late in the afternoon when we reached it, as this quarter is at a great distance from that in which we resided. The house was readily found; for there were still many curious persons looking up at the closed shutters from the opposite side of the way. It was an ordinary Parisian house with a gateway. Before going in, we walked up the street, turned down an *alley*, and then, again turning, passed in the *rear* of the building. Dupin,

---

premises, a building and the area of ground belonging to it
alley, a narrow street in a city
rear, back

meanwhile, examined the whole neighbourhood, as well as the house, paying attention to the smallest detail. I couldn't see any reason for this.

We went back to the front of the building and were
admitted by the agents in charge. We went upstairs – into the chamber where the body of Mademoiselle L'Espanaye had been found, and where both the

deceased still lay. I saw nothing beyond what had been stated in the 'Gazette des Tribuneaux'. Dupin examined everything carefully – not excepting the bodies of the victims. We then went into the other rooms and into the yard; a gendarme accompanying us throughout. The examinations occupied us until dark, when we took our departure. On our way home my companion stopped in for a moment at the office of one of the daily papers.

I have said that the unusual behaviour of my friend was something I had to put up with. He now stopped all conversation on the subject of the murder, until about noon the next day. He then asked me suddenly if I had observed anything peculiar at the scene of the crime.

There was something in the way he said the word 'peculiar' that made me *shudder*, I don't know why.

"No, nothing peculiar," I said; "nothing more, at least, than we both saw stated in the paper."

"The 'Gazette'," he replied, "has not entered, I fear, into the unusual horror of the thing. But let us forget the opinions of this print. It appears to me that this mystery is considered insoluble, for the very reason which should cause it to be regarded as easy of solution – I mean for its striking *characteristics*. The police are puzzled for the seeming lack of motive – not for the murder itself – but for such a cruel murder. They are puzzled, too, because voices were heard arguing, but no one was discovered upstairs but the dead body of

---

shudder, to temble for an instant with fear
characteristic, a distinguishing quality

25

Mademoiselle L'Espanaye, and there were no means of getting out of the house without being noticed by the party coming up the stairs. The wild disorder of the room; the corpse pushed up the chimney, with the head downward; the horrible way the body of the old lady was mutilated. These considerations, with those just mentioned, and others which I need not mention, have been enough to make the police unable to act. But in *investigations* such as the ones we are doing now, it should not be so much asked 'what has occurred,' as 'what has occurred that has never occurred before.' That which makes me arrive so easily at the solution of this mystery, is exactly what confuses the police."

I stared at him in astonishment.

"I am now awaiting," he continued, looking toward the door of our apartment – "I am now awaiting a person who, although he may not have committed these crimes, in some measure must have something to do with them. He is probably innocent of the worst part of the crimes committed. At least I hope so, for on this depends the solution of the entire mystery. I look for the man here – in this room – every moment. It is true that he may not arrive; but I am certain that he will. Should he come, it will be necessary to hold him back. Here are pistols; and we both know how to use them if it will be necessary."

I took the pistols, scarcely knowing what I did, or believing what I heard, while Dupin went on as if talking to himself. His eyes, empty of expression, regarded only the wall.

---

investigation, a careful examination or inquiry (into something)

"That the voices heard arguing," he said, "by the party on the stairs, were not the voices of the women themselves, was fully proved by the evidence. This relieves us of all doubt upon the question whether the old lady could have first destroyed the daughter, and afterwards killed herself. I speak of this point chiefly for the sake of method; for Madame L'Espanaye could not possibly have had the strength to push her daughter's corpse up the chimney as it was found. The nature of the wounds on her own person leaves out of consideration the idea of self-destruction. Murder, then, has been committed by some third party; and the voices of this third party were those heard arguing. Let me now turn the attention to what was peculiar in the *testimony*."

I remarked that, while all the witnesses agreed in supposing the gruff voice to be that of a Frenchman, they did not agree in regard to the shrill one.

"That was the evidence itself," said Dupin, "but it was not what was peculiar about the evidence. You have heard nothing special. Yet there was something to be observed. The witnesses, as you remark, agreed about the gruff voice. But in regard to the shrill voice what is peculiar is – not that they disagreed – but that, while an Italian, an Englishman, a Spaniard, a Dutchman, and a Frenchman attempted to describe it, each one spoke of it as that of a foreigner. Each is sure that it was not the voice of one of his countrymen. Each likens it – not to the voice of an individual of any nation with whose language he is familiar – but quite the con-

---

testimony, statement given to the police or in a law court

trary. The Frenchman supposes it to be the voice of a Spaniard, and 'might have distinguished some words had he been acquainted with the Spanish.' The Dutchman declares it to have been that of a Frenchman. But we find it stated that 'this witness does not understand any French.' The Englishman thinks it the voice of a German, and 'does not understand German.' The Spaniard is sure that it was that of an Englishman, but 'he has no knowledge of the English.' Now how strangely unusual must that voice have really been, to bring forward such testimony. I will now call your attention to three points. The voice is termed by one witness 'harsh rather than shrill.' It is represented by two others to have been 'quick and unusual.' No words – no sounds *resembling* words – were distinguished by any witness.

"I know not," continued Dupin, "what impression I may have made, so far, upon your own understanding. But I do not hesitate to say that this part of the testimony should form the basis of, and give direction to all farther progress in the investigations of the mystery. I will not say more yet, but the suspicion arisen was enough to give a definite form to my examinations of the chamber.

"Let us now move, in our imagination, to this chamber. What shall we first seek here? The means of getting out. It is not too much to say that neither of us believe in supernatural events. Madame and Mademoiselle L'Espanaye were not destroyed by spirits. The doers of the deed were material, and escaped

---

resemble, to be like

materially. Then how? Let us examine, each by each, the possible means of *exit*. It is clear that the murderers were in the room where Mademoiselle L'Espanaye was found, or at least in the room next to it, when the party came up the stairs. It is only from these two rooms that we have to seek the exit.

"The police have laid bare the floors, the ceilings, and the bricks of the walls in every direction. No secret exit could have escaped their attention. But, not trusting their eyes, I examined with my own. There were no secret means of getting out. Both doors leading from the rooms into the passage were *securely* locked, with the keyes inside. Let us turn to the chimneys. These, although of ordinary size will not admit throughout the whole passage, the body of a large cat. Then there are the windows left. Through those of the front room no one could have escaped without notice from the crowd in the street. The murderers must have passed, then, through those of the back room. Now, brought to this *conclusion* in the manner that we are, let us not refuse to accept it because it seems impossible. It is only left for us to prove that 'impossible' in reality it is not.

"There are two windows in the chamber. One of them has no furniture in front of it. The lower part of the other is hidden from view by the head of the bedstead which is put close up against it. The former was found securely fastened from within. It resisted the greatest force of those who tried to raise it. A hole had

---

exit, a way out
securely, safely
conclusion, a result arrived at by reasoning

been made in its frame to the left and a large nail was fitted into it, nearly to the head. Upon examining the other window, a *similar* nail was seen fitted in it in the same way; and an attempt to raise the *sash* failed also. The police were now entirely satisfied that exit had not been from these windows. And, therefore, it was not considered necessary to remove the nails and open them.

"My own examination was more particular, and was so for the reason I have just given because here it was, I knew, that what seemed impossible must be proved not to be so in reality.

"The murderers did escape from one of these windows. This being so, they could not have re-fastened the sashes from the inside, as they were found fastened. This consideration put a stop to the investigation of the police in this area. Yet the sashes were fastened. They must, then, have the power of fastening themselves. This was the only conclusion. I stepped to the free window, pulled out the nail with some difficulty, and attempted to raise the sash. It resisted all my efforts, as I had expected. A hidden *spring* must, I now knew, exist. I was certain of this, though I still couldn't explain the mystery of the nails. A careful search soon brought to light the hidden spring.

"I now replaced the nail and looked at it carefully. A person passing out through this window might have reclosed it, and the spring would have caught – but the

---

similar, alike in many ways
sash, sliding window frame holding the glass
spring, a mechanical part that returns to its original shape after being bent or pressed together

nail could not have been replaced. The conclusion was plain, and again narrowed my field of investigations. The murderers must have escaped through the other window. Supposing, then, the springs on each sash to be the same, as was probable, there must be found a difference between the nails, or at least between the manners in which they were fixed.

"I looked over the head-board of the empty bedstead at the second window. Passing my hand down behind the board, I discovered the spring without difficulty. It was, as I had supposed, *identical* to the first one. I now looked at the nail. It was as thick as the other, and fitted in the same manner driven in nearly up to the head.

"I had now *traced* the secret to its last and final result and that result was the nail. It had, I say, in every respect the appearance of its fellow in the other window. And here, at this point, ended the clue. 'There must be something wrong,' I said to myself, 'about the nail.' I touched it; and the head, with about a quarter of the *shank*, came off in my fingers. The rest of the shank was still in the hole, where it had been broken off. I looked at it carefully. It had probably been broken some time ago as there was *rust* on the surfaces; and probably with a blow of a *hammer* as the head of

hammer

---

identical, the same in every way
trace, to follow back or study in detail or step by step
shank, the long straight part of a nail
rust, the reddish-brown substance which can form on iron

the nail had cut into the top of the bottom sash and remained fastened there. I now carefully replaced the head of the nail in the little *notch* from which I had taken it, and it looked completely like a perfect nail. Pressing the spring I gently raised the sash for a few inches; the head went up with it, sitting in the notch. I closed the window, and again it looked like a whole nail.

"I had found the answer to the puzzle, so far. The murderer had escaped through the window where the bedstead stood. Dropping of its own accord upon his exit (or perhaps purposely closed), it had become fastened by the spring. It was this spring that had kept the window firmly closed, not the nail, as the police had believed.

"The next question is how did the murderers descend. Upon this point I had been satisfied in my walk with you around the building. About five feet and a half from the window in question there runs a *lightning-rod*. From this rod it would have been possible to reach one of the shutters. We saw them from the rear of the house, they were about half open – this is to say, they stood off at right angles from the wall. The police, having satisfied themselves that no exit could have been made from the windows, only made a very rapid examination of the rear of the house, and did not give this point any consideration.

---

notch, a V-shaped cut
lightning, flash of electricity between clouds or from a cloud to earth during a storm
lightning-rod, (American) lightning-conductor, a metal rod fixed to the highest point of a building and connected to the earth as a protection against lightning

"It was clear to me, however, that the shutter belonging to the window at the head of the bed, would, if swung fully back to the wall, reach to within two feet of the lightning-rod. By employing a very unusual activity and courage, it is possible to enter the window from the rod by taking a firm grab on the shutter and swinging oneself into the room if we imagine the window open at the time.

"I wish you to bear in mind that I have spoken of a very unusual degree of activity necessary to succeed in such a difficult task. I want to show you first, that the thing might possibly have been done. But, secondly and chiefly, I wish you to understand fully the very extraordinary character of that skill which could have done it.

"Now, put together the very unusual activity of which I have just spoken, and that very peculiar shrill and unequal voice, about whose nationality no two persons could be found to agree."

At these words some half-formed idea of the meaning of Dupin quickly went through my mind, but I was not able to understand it. My friend went on.

"You will see," he said, "that I now talk of entrance instead of exit. I suggest that both were effected in the same manner, at the same point. Let's now return to the room and look at the appearances here. The chest of drawers had been searched. The articles found in the drawers were probably all there had ever been. Madame L'Espanaye and her daughter lived a very retired life – saw no company – seldom went out – had no need for many clothes. Those found were at least of as good a quality as any likely to be possessed by these ladies. If a thief had taken any, why did he not take the best why did he not take all? In a word, why did he leave four thousand francs in gold, in bags, on the floor? No, it was not a thief who committed these crimes.

"Keeping now in mind the points to which I have drawn your attention – that peculiar voice, that unusual climbing skill, and the absence of a motive in a murder so horrible as this – let us glance at the killing itself. Here is a woman strangled to death by the strength of hands, and pushed up a chimney, head downward. Ordinary murderers do not kill this way. Think, too, how great must have been that strength which could have done this. It took several persons to drag the body down!

"On the floor of the fireplace were thick tresses of grey human hair. These had been torn out by the roots. You realize the great force necessary in tearing thus from the head even twenty or thirty hairs together.

"The throat of the old lady was not merely cut, but the head absolutely separated from the body: the instrument was a mere razor. The bruises on the body of Madame L'Espanaye were caused by the stone pavement of the yard, upon which the victim had fallen from the window which looked in upon the bed. This idea, however simple it may now seem, escaped the police. Their minds were completely closed to the possibility of the windows having been opened at all because of the nails.

"Now, if you also consider the odd disorder of the chamber and combine it with the ideas of surprising climbing skills, a superhuman strength, a horrible murder without a motive, and a voice foreign in tone to the ears of men of many nations. What result has come forward? What impression have I made upon your imagination?

I felt a creeping in the flesh as Dupin asked me the question. "A madman," I said, "has done this deed."

"But the voices of madmen," he replied, "even in their wildest expressions, could never match that peculiar voice heard upon the stairs. Madmen are of some nation, and their language, however impossible to understand, have sounds that can be distinguished. Besides, the hair of a madman is not such as I now hold in my hand. This *tuft* of hair I took from the *clutched* hand of Madame L'Espanaye. Tell me what you can make of it."

"Dupin!" I said astonished; "this hair is most unusual – this is no human hair."

"I have not said that it is," said he; "but before we decide this point, I wish you to glance at this little *sketch* I have made on this paper. It is an exact copy of the dark bruises of the fingerprints on the throat of Mademoiselle L'Espanaye. As you can see," continued my friend, spreading out the paper on the table before us, "this drawing gives the idea of a firm and fixed hold. Try now to place all your fingers, at the same time, in the impressions as you see them."

I tried in vain.

"This is not the mark," I said, "of a human hand."

"Read now this passage," replied Dupin, handing me a piece of paper.

---

tuft, a number of similar things growing together like hair, grass or the like
clutched, firmly, tightly closed
sketch, a rough drawing

It was a description of the large *orang-utan* of the East Indian Islands. I understood the full horror of the murders at once.

"The description of the *digits*," I said, as I made an end of the reading, "is in exact agreement with this drawing. I see that no animal but an orang-utan, as it is described here, could have made the marks as you have drawn them. This tuft of hair, too, is identical in character with that of the beast. But I cannot possibly understand the particulars of this mystery. Two voices were heard, and one of them was, beyond any doubt, the voice of a Frenchman."

"True; and you will remember the expression he was heard saying, 'mon Dieu!' A Frenchman knew about the murder. It is possible – indeed it is far more than probable – that he was *innocent* of having taken any part in these crimes. The orang-utan may have escaped from him. He may have traced it to the chamber; but during the events that followed, he could never have caught it again. It is still *at large*. Well, I will not continue these guesses. If the Frenchman in question is indeed innocent – as I suppose – this advertisement will bring him to our residence. I left it last night, upon our return home, at the office of 'Le Monde', a paper with interest in shipping and much read by sailors."

He handed me a paper, and I read the following:
CAUGHT – In the Bois de Boulogne*, early in the

---

orang-utan, a large reddish-brown *ape* from Borneo or Sumatra, see page 41
digit, a finger or toe
innocent, not guilty (of a crime)
at large, free
*a large park – in those days outside Paris

morning of the – (the morning of the murders,) a very
large orang-utan. The owner, a sailor belonging to a
Maltese ship, may have the animal again, upon paying a few charges arising from its keeping. Call at
No. – , Rue – , Faubourg St Germain – third floor.

"How was it possible," I asked, "that you should
know the man to be a sailor, and belonging to a Maltese ship?"

"I do not know it," said Dupin. "I am not sure of it.
Here, however, is a small piece of *ribbon*, which from
its appearance has been used in tying the hair in one
of those long tails which sailors are so fond of.
Moreover, this knot is one which few besides sailors
can tie, and is peculiar to the Maltese. I picked the ribbon up at the foot of the lightning-rod. It could not
have belonged to either of the deceased. Now, if after
all I am wrong in supposing that the Frenchman was a
sailor belonging to a Maltese ship, still I can have
done no harm in saying what I did in the advertisement. He will not take the trouble to find out why. But
if I am right, a great point is gained. Knowing of the
murder, although innocent, the Frenchman will naturally hesitate about replying to the advertisement –
about demanding the orang-utan. He will reason
thus: 'I am innocent; I am poor; my orang-utan is of
great value. Why should I lose it now? It was found in
the Bois de Boulogne – far away from the scene of the
crime. How can it ever be suspected that a beast
should have done the deed? Should the police even
trace the animal, it would be impossible to prove that I

---

ribbon, a narrow strip of material used in tying hair etc.

had anything to do with the murder. I will answer the advertisement, get the orang-utan, and keep it close until this matter has blown over.'"

At this moment we heard a step upon the stairs.

"Be ready," said Dupin, "with your pistols, but neither use them nor show them until at a signal from myself." The front door of the house had been left open, and the visitor had entered, without ringing, and advanced several steps upon the staircase. Now, however, he seemed to hesitate. Then we heard him descending. Dupin was moving quickly to the door, when we again heard him coming up. He did not turn back a second time, but stepped up with decision and knocked quickly at the door of our chamber.

"Come in," said Dupin, heartily.

A man entered. He was a sailor – one could see that – tall and strong, with a greatly sunburnt face. He bowed and said 'good evening' to us.

"Sit down, my friend," said Dupin. "I suppose you have called about the orang-utan. A remarkably fine, and no doubt valuable animal. How old do you think he is?"

The sailor drew a long breath of relief, and then replied:

"I have no way of telling – but he can't be more than four or five years old. Have you got him here?"

"Oh no, we couldn't keep him here. He is at a *stable* in the Rue Dubourg, just by. You can get him in the morning."

"I don't mean that you should be at all this trouble

---

stable, a building in which horses or other animals are kept

for nothing, sir," said the man. "Couldn't expect it. Am very willing to pay a reward for the finding of the animal – that is to say, anything within reason."

"Well," replied my friend, "that is all very fair, to be sure. Let me think! what should I have? Oh! I will tell you. My reward shall be this. You shall give me all the information in your power about these murders in the Rue Morgue."

Dupin said the last words in a very low tone, and very quietly, too, he walked towards the door, locked it, and put the key in his pocket. He then drew out his pistol and placed it, calmly, on the table.

The sailor's face went red, and he started to his feet. But the next moment he fell back into his seat, trembling violently, and with the face of death itself. He didn't speak a word. I pitied him from the bottom of my heart.

"My friend," said Dupin, in a kind tone, "you don't have to be afraid – you really don't. We mean you no harm whatever. Upon my honour, as a gentleman and as a Frenchman, I assure you that. I know perfectly well that you are innocent of the horrible crimes in the Rue Morgue. But we know, however, that you are in some measure *implicated* in them. From what I have already said, you must know that I have means of which you could never have dreamed. Now the thing stands thus. You have done nothing which you could have avoided – nothing, certainly, which makes you guilty. You have nothing to hide and no reason to do so. On the other hand, you are bound by your honour to confess all you know."

"So help me God," the sailor said, after a short pause, "I will tell you all I know about this affair; – but I do not expect you to believe one half I say – I would be a fool indeed if I did. Still I am innocent, and I will *make a clean breast* if I die for it."

What he stated was, in substance, this. He had lately made *voyage* to the Indian *Archipelago*. A party, of which he formed one, landed at Borneo. Himself and a companion caught the orang-utan in the forest and managed to bring it on the ship. His companion dying, the *ferocious* animal fell into his possession alone. After a difficult home voyage, he succeeded in

---

implicated in, having something to do with
make a clean breast, to confess fully
voyage, a long journey by sea
archipelago, a group of islands
ferocious, extremely fierce and violent

bringing it to Paris to his residence. Here he kept it locked up in a small room, not to attract towards himself the unpleasant curiosity of the neighbours. His plan was to sell it.

Returning home after a merry night with other sailors, on the night, or rather in the morning of the murder, he found the beast occupying his own bedroom, into which it had broken. Razor in hand, it was sitting in front of a looking-glass, trying to shave, something which it no doubt had watched its master do on several occasions. *Terrified* at the sight of so dangerous a weapon in the possession of an animal so ferocious, the man, for some moments, was at a loss what to do. He had been accustomed, however, to quieten the creature by the use of a *whip* and he decided to do this again. On the sight of the whip, the orang-utan sprang at once through the door of the chamber, down the stairs, and from there, through an open window into the street.

The Frenchman followed in despair. The *ape*, razor still in hand, occasionally stopped and waved the razor at him, until he had nearly come up with it. It then again made off. In this manner the chase continued for a long time. The streets were quiet, as it was nearly three o'clock in the morning. In passing down an alley in the rear of the Rue Morgue, the ape's attention was arrested by a light shining from the open window of Madame L'Espanaye's chamber, in the fourth

---

terrified, very frightened
whip, a long narrow strip of leather with a handle, used for driving horses or for punishment
ape, a kind of very large monkey

story of her house. Rushing to the building, it saw the lightning-rod, climbed up with incredible ease, grabbed the shutter, which was thrown fully back against the wall, and swung itself directly upon the headboard of the bed. It didn't take more than a minute. The shutter was kicked open again by the orang-utan as it entered the room.

The sailor, now, had strong hopes of recapturing the beast. It could only escape from the trap into which it had climbed, by means of the rod, and he could catch it as it came down. On the other hand, there was much cause for anxiety as to what it might do in the house. The thought of this made the man follow the ape. He went up the rod without much difficulty, being a sailor. But, when he had arrived as high as the window, which lay far to his left, he was stopped. All he could do was to reach over and try to get a *glimpse* of the *interior* of the room. At this glimpse he nearly fell from his hold through horror. It was then that those terrible screams began, which had awoken the inhabitants of the Rue Morgue. Madame L'Espanaye and her daughter, dressed in their night clothes, had been arranging some papers in the iron box already mentioned. It was open, and its contents lay beside it on the floor. The victims must have been sitting with their backs toward the window.

As the sailor looked in, the huge animal had seized Madame L'Espanaye by the hair, (which was loose, as she had been combing it,) and was moving the razor

---

glimpse, a brief look
interior, the inside (of something)

about her face as if trying to shave her. The daughter lay motionless on the floor; she had fainted. The screams and struggles of the old lady (during which the hair was torn from her head) had the effect of changing the probably peaceful purposes of the orang-utan into those of violent anger. With one determined sweep of its strong arm it nearly *severed* the

---

sever, to remove by cutting

head from the body. At the sight of blood the beast became even more violent, and flashing fire from its eyes, it flew upon the body of the girl. With its horrible hands firmly grabbed around her throat, it strangled her. Its wild glances fell at this moment at the face of its master outside the window. The anger of the beast, who no doubt still bore in mind the whip, immediately turned into fear. As if it wanted to hide its bloody deeds, it jumped nervously about the chamber, throwing down and breaking the furniture as it moved, and dragging the bed from the bedstead. Finally, it seized first the corpse of the daughter, and pushed it up the chimney, as it was found; then that of the old lady, which it threw out of the window.

As the ape approached the window with the mutilated corpse, the sailor climbed back on to the rod and went down as quickly as he could. He then hurried home, leaving the orang-utan to its fate, fearing he would be connected with the murders. The words heard by the party on the staircase were the Frenchman's exclamations of horror, mixed with the shrill sounds made by the ape.

I have scarcely anything to add. The orang-utan must have escaped from the chamber, by the rod, just before the breaking of the door. It must have closed the window as it passed through it. It was later caught by the owner himself, who sold it for a large sum of money to a zoo. Le Bon was instantly *released* after we had given a full account of the events to the police. The Inspector of police, however, was not altogether

---

release, to set free

satisfied at the turn affairs had taken and remarked how much more proper it would be if every person minded his own business.

"Let him talk," said Dupin, who had not thought it necessary to reply. "I am satisfied with having defeated him in his own castle."

The Gold-*Bug*

bug

Many years ago, a close friendship between Mr William Legrand and myself was established. He was of a distinguished, old French family*, and had once been wealthy; but sad events had made him very poor. He left New Orleans, the city of his family, and took up residence at Sullivan's Island, near Charleston, South Carolina.

This island is a very unusual one. It consists of little else than sea sand, and is about three miles long, and at no point more than a quarter of a mile broad. It is separated from the mainland by a narrow stream of water, running slowly through a *wilderness* of *reeds*. The whole island, with the exception of the area occupied by Fort Moultry and a line of hard, white beach on the sea coast, is covered with thick bushes of sweet *myrtle* and the air is heavy with its *fragrance*.

On this island Legrand had built himself a small *hut*, which he occupied when – by accident – I first met him. We soon became friends. He was a very interesting man, well educated, with unusual powers of the

---

*New Orleans was founded by the French in 1718
wilderness, desert or wild area of a country
reed, a kind of tall, stiff grass growing on wet ground
myrtle, a woody evergreen plant with rosy or white flowers
fragrance, sweet smell
hut, a small, simple house

mind, but often suffering from a dark *mood*. He had with him many books, but seldom read any. He spent most of his time hunting and fishing, or strolling along the beach and through the myrtles, looking for shells or rare insects. His collection of the latter was very large and interesting.

On these trips he was usually accompanied by an old negro, called Jupiter, who had been given free a long time ago but who insisted on accompanying his '*Massa* Will' wherever he went.

The winters on Sullivan's island are seldom very severe, and in the *fall* of the year it is a rare event indeed when a fire is considered necessary. About the middle of October 18 – , some rather cold days occurred however. Just before sunset I made my way through the evergreens to the hut of my friend, whom I had not visited for several weeks. At that time I had my residence in Charleston, a distance of nine miles from the Island.

Upon reaching the house I knocked, as was my custom. Getting no reply, I sought for the key where I knew it was hidden, unlocked the door and went in. A fine fire was burning. I was surprised but also very pleased. I threw off my overcoat, took an arm-chair by the fire, and awaited patiently the arrival of my hosts.

Soon after dark they arrived, and gave me a very warm welcome. Jupiter, grinning from ear to ear, busied himself cooking supper. Legrand was in a very happy mood. He had hunted down and caught, with

---

mood, state of mind
massa, master
fall, (Am.) autumn

the help of Jupiter, a *scarabæus* which he believed to be totally new. He wished to have my opinion on it the next day.

"And why not to-night?" I asked, rubbing my hands over the fire, and wishing the whole tribe of scarabæi to the devil.

"Ah, if I had only known you were here!" said Legrand, "but it's so long since I saw you. And how could I know that you would pay me a visit this very night of all others? As I was coming home I met an officer from Fort Moultrie, a friend of mine sharing my interest in insects. I lent him the bug; so it will be impossible for you to see it until morning. Stay here to-night, and I will send Jupiter down for it at sunrise. It's very lovely, of a *brilliant* gold colour about the size of a large nut with two black spots near the top of the back, and another, somewhat longer, at the bottom. The *antennæ* are – "

"De* bug is a goole** bug, solid every bit of him, inside and all – never felt half so heavy a bug in my life," Jupiter interrupted.

"Well, I suppose it is, Jup," replied Legrand. "The colour" – here he turned to me – "is really almost enough to support Jupiter's idea. You never saw a more golden shine. But of this you cannot judge until to-morrow. In the meantime I can give you some idea of the shape." Saying this, he seated himself at a small

---

scarabæus, plural *scarabæi,* (Latin) beetle
brilliant, very bright
antennae, the hair-shaped feelers on the heads of insects
**the*
***gold*

table, on which were a pen and *ink*, but no paper. He looked for some in the drawer, but found none.

"Never mind," he said at length, "this will answer," and he drew from his pocket a piece of dirty paper, and made upon it a rough drawing with the pen.

While he did this, I remained in my chair by the fire. When the drawing was complete, he handed it to me without rising. As I received it, a loud *growl* was heard outside the door. Jupiter opened it and a large Newfoundland*, belonging to Legrand, rushed in, leaped on my shoulders, and greeted me fondly; for I had shown him much attention during previous visits.

---

ink, black or coloured liquid used in writing
growl, a deep sound made by a dog
*a kind of dog

When he was finally quiet, I looked at the paper, and, to speak the truth, found myself not a little puzzled at what my friend had drawn.

"Well," I said, after looking at it for some minutes, "this is a strange scarabæus, I must confess, new to me: never saw anything like it before – unless it was a *skull*, or a death's-head – which it looks more like than anything else that has come under my observation."

skull

"A death's-head!" exclaimed Legrand – "Oh – yes – well, it has something of that appearance on paper, no doubt. The two upper black spots look like eyes, eh? and the longer one at the bottom like a mouth."

"Perhaps so," I said; "but, Legrand, I fear you are no artist. I must wait until I see the beetle itself, if I am to form any idea of its appearance."

"Well, I don't know," said he, a little angry, "I draw quite well, I should think."

"But, my dear fellow, you are joking then," said I, "this is an excellent drawing of a skull – and your scarabæus must be the strangest scarabæus in the world if it looks like it. And where are the antennæ you spoke of?"

"The antennæ!" said Legrand, who seemed to be getting unusually warm on the subject; "I am sure you must see the antennæ, I made them as *distinct* as they

---

distinct, easily seen (or heard)

are in the original insect."

"Well, well," I said, "perhaps you have – still I don't see them;" and I handed him back the paper. I was much surprised at the turn affairs had taken; his bad mood puzzled me – and as for the drawing of the beetle, there were absolutely no antennæ to be seen, and the whole did look very much like that of a death's-head.

He received the paper, and was about to throw it into the fire, when something caught his attention. In an instant his face grew violently red – and in another extremely pale. For some minutes he continued to examine the drawing where he sat. At length he rose, took a candle from the table, and crossed the room. He seated himself at a writing-desk in the farthest corner of the room. Here again he made a careful examination of the paper, turning it in all directions. He said nothing, however, and his behaviour greatly astonished me. I found it best to say nothing. After a while he placed the paper in a drawer, which he locked.

It had been my intention to pass the night at the hut, as I had frequently done before, but, seeing my host in this mood, I thought it proper to take leave. He did not press me to remain, but shook my hand warmly as I left.

It was about a month after this (during which time I had seen nothing of Legrand) when I received a visit, at Charleston, from his man, Jupiter. I had never seen the good old negro look so unhappy, and I feared something terrible had happened to my friend.

"Well, Jup," said I, "how is your master?"

"Why, to speak the truth, massa, him not so very well."

"Not well! I am truly sorry to hear it. What does he complain of?"

"Him never complain of noffin* – but him very sick for all dat**."

"Very sick, Jupiter! – why didn't you say so at once? Is he in bed?"

"No, dat he aint***. Massa Will say noffin is de matter with him – but den what make him go about looking dis here way, with de head down and his face white?"

"What has caused this illness, or rather this change of behaviour? Has anything happened since I saw you?"

"No, massa, noffin since den – it was before den, I'm afraid – it was de very day you was dare****."

"How, what do you mean?"

"Why, massa, I mean de bug."

"The what?"

"De bug – I'm very certain dat massa Will been bit somewhere about de head by dat goole-bug."

"And you think that the bite made him sick?"

"I don't think noffin about it – I know it. What make him dream about de goole so much, if it aint cause he been bit by de goole-bug?"

"But how do you know he dreams about gold?"

"How I know? why cause he talk about it in de sleep – dat's how I know."

---

*nothing
**that
***isn't
****there

"Well, Jup, perhaps you are right. Did you bring any message from Mr Legrand?"

Jupiter handed me a note which read:

MY DEAR –

Why have I not seen you for so long a time? I hope you have not been so foolish as to *take offence* at my bad mood.

Since I saw you I have had great cause for concern. I have something to tell you, yet I don't know how to tell it, or whether I should tell it at all.

I have not been quite well for some days. If you can, in any way, make it convenient, come over with Jupiter. Do come. I wish to see you tonight, upon business of importance. I assure you that it is of the highest importance.

Ever yours,

WILLIAM LEGRAND

There was something in the tone of this note which made me feel uneasy. The whole style was so different from that of Legrand. What could he be dreaming of? What "business of the highest importance" could he possibly have? Without hesitating I therefore prepared to accompany the negro.

When we reached the boat I noticed a *scythe* and three *spades*, all new, lying in the bottom.

"What is the meaning of all this, Jup?" I inquired.

"Massa Will told me to buy dem for him in de town."

---

take offence, to become hurt and angry
scythe, spade, see page 54

scythe

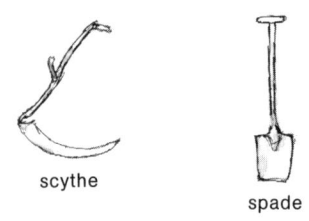

spade

"But what is your 'Massa Will' going to do with scythes and spades?"

"Dat's more dan I know. But it's all come of de bug."

Finding that Jupiter could not satisfy my curiosity, his whole mind being filled with "de bug", I now stepped into the boat and made sail.

With a fair wind we soon ran into the little bay north of Fort Moultrie, and a walk of some two miles brought us to the hut. It was about three in the afternoon when we arrived. Legrand had been awaiting us eagerly. He grabbed my hand and shook it nervously. His face was pale, and his deep-set eyes shone in an unusual way.

After some inquiries about his health, I asked him, not knowing what better to say, if he had got the scarabæus back from his friend at Fort Moultrie.

"Oh, yes," he said, "I got it from him the next morning. I shall never part with that scarabæus again. Do you know that Jupiter is quite right about it?"

"In what way?" I asked, sad at heart.

"In supposing it to be a bug of real gold." He looked at me seriously, and I felt deeply shocked.

"This bug is to make my fortune," he continued with a smile, "to get me back my family possessions. Is it any wonder, then, that I prize it? Since Fortune has thought fit that I should have it, I have only to use it properly, and it will show me how I shall arrive at the gold."

Legrand rose, with a grave air, and brought me the beetle from a glass case. It was a beautiful scarabæus, and, at that time unknown – of course a great prize in a scientific point of view. There were two round, black spots near the top of the back, and a long one near the bottom. The *scales* were extremely hard and shone like polished gold. The insect was very heavy, and, taking all things into consideration, I could hardly blame Jupiter for his opinion about it; but why Legrand agreed with that opinion, I could not, for the life of me, tell.

"I sent for you," he said, in a grave voice, when I had completed my examination of the beetle, "I sent for you, because I need your assistance. Jupiter and myself are going on an *expedition* into the hills, on the mainland, and, in this expedition, we shall need the help of a person whom we can trust. Whether we succeed or fail, the excitement which you now feel in me will be relieved."

"I am anxious to help you in any way," I replied, "but do you mean to say that this *infernal* beetle has any connection with your expedition into the hills?"

"It has."

"Then, Legrand, I shall certainly not come. You shall go to bed, and I will remain with you a few days, until

---

scales, here, the thin, hard plates that cover and protect the fine wings
expedition, journey by a group of persons for a particular purpose
infernal, word to express anger

you get over this. You are not well. You have a fever –"

"You are mistaken," he interrupted, "I am as well as I can expect to be under the excitement which I suffer. If you really wish me well, you will relieve this excitement. And if you will not, then I am very sorry – for we shall have to try it by ourselves."

"Try it by yourselves! The man is surely mad! – but wait! – how long do you propose to be absent?"

"Probably all night. We shall start immediately, and be back, at all events, by sunrise."

"And will you promise me, upon your honour, that when the bug business (good God!) is settled to your satisfaction, you will return home and follow my advice and go to bed and rest?"

"Yes, I promise; and let us be off, for we have no time to lose."

With a heavy heart I accompanied my friend. We started about four o'clock – Legrand, Jupiter, the dog, and myself. Jupiter had with him the scythe and spades – he was most unhappy; "dat d-d bug" were the only words which escaped his lips during the journey. For my own part, I had charge of a couple of *lanterns,* while Legrand took care of the scarabæus, which he carried attached to the end of a bit of string that he was swinging in front of him as he went. He was unwilling

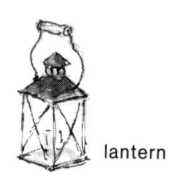

lantern

---

lantern, a case with windows for carrying a candle

to answer any of my questions as to the object of the expedition; the only words I received in reply were "we shall see!"

We crossed the water at the head of the island, and, climbing the high grounds on the shore of the mainland, continued in a northwesterly direction. We went through an extemely wild and lonely part of the country, where no *trace* of a human footstep was to be seen. Legrand led the way with decision; pausing only for an instant, here and there, to find what appeared to be certain landmarks put there by himself on a former occasion.

In this manner we journeyed for about two hours, and the sun was just setting when we entered an area far more dark and dull than any yet seen. It was a flat

---

trace, mark or sign left by someone or something

piece of land, near the top of a high hill. Bushes and trees grew everywhere from bottom to top. Spread all over were large rocks that appeared to lie loosely upon the soil, prevented only from falling down into the valley below by the support of the trees against which they rested.

The natural platform to which we had climbed was thickly overgrown with *brambles*, through which it would have been impossible for us to force our way but for the scythe. Jupiter, by direction of his master, cleared for us a path to the foot of an enormously tall *tulip-tree*, surrounded by some eight or ten oaks. It was much taller and more beautiful than them all, and all other trees that I had ever seen.

When we reached this tree, Legrand turned to Jupiter, and asked him if he thought he could climb it. The old man seemed astonished by the question, and for some moments made no reply. At length he approached the huge trunk, walked slowly around it, and examined it with attention.

"Yes, massa," he answered, "Jup climb any tree he ever see in his life."

"Then up with you as soon as possible, for it will soon be too dark to see what we are about."

"How far must I go up, massa?" inquired Jupiter.

"Get up the main trunk first, and then I will tell you which way to go – and here – stop! take this beetle with you."

"De bug, Massa Will! – de goole bug!" cried the negro, drawing back.

"If you are afraid, Jup, a great big negro like you, to take hold of a harmless little dead beetle, why you can carry it up by this string – but, if you do not take it up

tulip-tree

brambles

with you in some way, I shall find it necessary to break your head with this spade."

"What de matter now, massa?" said Jup, "always want *to raise fuss* with old nigger. Was only funny anyhow. Me afraid of de bug!" He took hold of the extreme end of the string, and, holding the insect as far from his person as he could, prepared to climb the tree.

The tulip-tree, or Liriodendron Tulipiferum, is the most splendid tree of the American forest. It often rises to a great height without branches, but with age, the trunk becomes uneven and smaller branches stick out. Jupiter put his arms around the huge trunk and seized with his hands some *projections*, resting his naked toes on others. After one or two narrow escapes from falling, he at length *wriggled* himself into the first great fork.

"Which way must I go now, Massa Will?" he asked.

"Keep up the largest branch – the one on this side," said Legrand. The negro climbed higher and higher, until he could not be seen anymore. After a while his voice was heard.

"How much further must I go?"

"Look down the trunk and count the branches below you on this side. How many branches have you passed?"

"One, two, three, four, five – I done pass five big branches, massa."

---

raise fuss, here, to make trouble for
projection, that which sticks out
wriggle, to move the body from one side to the other

"Then go one branch higher."

In a few minutes the voice was heard again, announcing that the seventh branch was reached.

"Now, Jup," cried Legrand, very excited, "I want you to work your way out on that branch as far as you can. If you see anything strange, let me know."

By this time what little doubt I might have had of my friends madness, was put finally to rest. The man was crazy, and I became seriously anxious about getting him home. While I was wondering what was best to do, Jupiter's voice was again heard.

"I fear to go far out on dis branch – tis* dead branch pretty much all the way."

"Did you say it was a dead branch, Jupiter?" cried Legrand in an excited voice.

"Yes, massa."

"Try the wood well, then, with your knife, and see if you think it very *rotten*."

"Him rotten, massa, sure enough," replied the negro in a few moments, "but not so very rotten. Can go out a little bit by myself, dat's true."

"By yourself! What do you mean?"

"Why I mean de bug. Tis very heavy bug. Suppose I drop him down, and den de branch won't break, with just de weight of one nigger."

"You infernal *scoundrel*!" cried Legrand, much relieved, "what do you mean by telling me such nonsense as that? As sure as you let that beetle fall! – I'll break your neck. Look here, Jupiter! Do you hear me?"

---

*it's
rotten, of wood, so bad that it will break into small pieces
scoundrel, very bad person

"Yes, massa, needn't *hollo* at poor nigger dat way."

"Well, now listen! – if you will go out on the branch as far as you think safe, and not let go of the beetle, I'll make you a present of a silver dollar as soon as you get down."

"I'm going, Massa Will – almost out to de end now."

"Out to the end!" here fairly screamed Legrand, "do you say you are out to the end of that branch?"

"Soon be to de end, massa, – o-o-o-o-oh! What is dis here on de tree?"

"Well!" cried Legrand, highly delighted, "what is it?"

"Why it aint noffin but a skull – somebody left him head up de tree, and the birds took every bit of meat off."

"A skull, you say! – very well! – how is it fastened to the branch? – what holds it on?"

"Sure enough, massa, dare's a great big nail in de skull."

"Well now, Jupiter, do exactly as I tell you – do you hear?"

"Yes, massa."

"Pay attention, then! – find the left eye of the scull. Do you know your right hand from your left?"

There was a long pause. At length the negro asked, "Is de left eye of de skull on de same side as de left hand of de skull, too? – cause de skull aint got not a bit of hand at all – never mind! I got de left eye now – here de left eye! What must I do with it?"

"Let the little beetle drop through it, as far as the string will reach – but be careful and not let go your hold of the string."

---

holler, to shout

"All dat done, Massa Will; very easy to put de bug through de hole – look out for him down below!"

No part of Jupiter's person could be seen, but the beetle was now seen shining at the end of the string, like a ball of gold, in the last rays of the setting sun. The scarabæus hung quite clear of any branches, and, if allowed to fall, would have fallen at our feet. Legrand immediately took the scythe, and cleared with it a circular space, just beneath the insect. Having done so, he ordered Jupiter to let go of the string and come down from the tree.

Driving a *peg* into the ground, at the precise spot where the beetle fell, my friend now produced from his pocket a *tape-measure*. Fastening one end of this at that point of the trunk of the tree which was nearest the peg, he unrolled it till it reached the peg. He then continued to unroll it, in the direction already established by the two points of the tree and the peg, for the distance of fifty feet while Jupiter cleared away the brambles with the scythe. At the spot thus reached, a second peg was driven into the ground. About this, as a centre, a circle about four feet in diameter was described. Taking now a spade himself, and giving one to Jupiter and one to me, Legrand begged us to begin digging as quickly as possible.

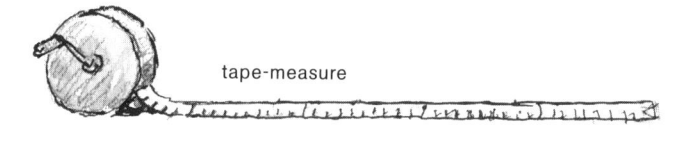

tape-measure

---

peg, short, not very thick piece of wood or metal used to fasten or mark something

To speak the truth, it did not amuse me, and I would have been glad to refuse; for the night was coming on, and I felt extremely tired from the exercise already taken. But I saw no way of escape, and did not want to upset my friend's mind. He had, no doubt, taken faith in some of the many Southern tales about money buried, and his ideas had been confirmed by the finding of the scarabæus. I was sad and puzzled, but, at length I thought it best to dig with a good will.

We dug for two hours, by the lights of the lanterns. We had reached five feet down, and yet there were no signs of any treasure. We all took a pause, and I began to hope that this stupid affair was at an end. Legrand, however, picked up the spade and started digging again. We had *excavated* the entire circle, and went another two feet down. Still nothing appeared. Legrand was deeply disappointed, and began, slowly, to put on his coat, which he had thrown off at the beginning of the work. In the meantime I made no remark. Jupiter, at a signal from his master, began to gather up his tools. We freed the dog which had been tied to the tree during the whole operation, and turned in deep silence towards home.

We had taken, perhaps, a dozen steps in this direction, when Legrand suddenly stopped and seized Jupiter by the collar. The astonished negro opened his eyes and mouth wide, let fall the spades, and fell upon his knees.

"You scoundrel," said Legrand, "you infernal black scoundrel! – speak, I tell you! – answer me this instant,

---

excavate, to dig out a hole

which – which is your left eye?"

"Oh, my *golly*, Massa Will! aint dis here my left eye for certain?" cried Jupiter, placing his hand on his right eye.

"I thought so! – I knew it! – hurrah!" cried Legrand, letting the negro go. "Come, we must go back; the game's not up yet!" and he again led the way to the tulip-tree.

"Jupiter," he said, when we reached its foot, "come here! Was the skull nailed to the branch with the face outward, or with the face to the *limb*?"

"De face was out, massa, so dat de birds could get to

---

golly, mild exclamation of surprise
limb, branch

the eyes good, without any trouble."

"Well, then, was it this eye or that through which you let the beetle fall?" here Legrand touched each of Jupiter's eyes.

"It was dis eye, massa – de left eye – just as you tell me," and here it was his right eye that the negroe pointed at.

"That will do – we must try it again."

Here my friend removed the peg which marked the spot where the beetle fell, to a spot about three inches to the westward of its former position. Taking, now, the tape-measure from the nearest point of the trunk to the peg, as before, and continuing in a straight line to the distance of fifty feet, a spot was reached which was several yards from the point at which we had been digging.

Around the new position a circle, somewhat larger than the first, was now described, and we again set to work with the spades. I was dreadfully tired, but, hardly understanding what had caused the change in my thoughts, I had become most interested, even excited. I dug eagerly, and now and then caught myself actually looking for the fancied treasure.

When we had been at work perhaps an hour and a half, we were interrupted by the violent *howlings* of the dog. Jupiter tried to silence him, but he made violent resistance, and leaping into the hole, it had uncovered, in a few seconds, a mass of human bones. One or two strokes of a spade upturned a large Spanish knife, several buttons of metal, and, as we dug farther, three

---

howling, a loud, long sound like that of a wolf

or four loose pieces of gold and silver coins came to light.

At the sight of these Jupiter cried out in joy, but his master looked extremely disappointed. He urged us, however, to continue our efforts. He had hardly said this when I *stumbled* and fell forward, having caught the toe of my boot in a large ring of iron that lay buried in the loose earth.

We now worked in earnest, and never did I pass ten minutes of more *intense* excitement. During this period we had almost dug up a *chest* of wood which was perfectly preserved. This box was three feet and a half long, three feet broad, and two and a half feet deep. It was firmly secured by bands of iron. On each side of the chest, near the top, were three rings of iron – six in all – by means of which six persons would be able to get a firm hold. We at once saw that it would be impossible to remove so great a weight. Luckily, the lid was fastened only with two sliding *bolts*. These we drew back – trembling with anxiety. In an instant, a treasure of enormous value of gold and jewels lay before us flashing in the light of the lanterns.

I cannot describe the feelings with which I *gazed*. Legrand was silent with excitement. Jupiter's face became as deadly pale as it is possible, in the nature of things, for a negro to become. Then he fell upon his

---

stumble, to strike the foot against something and lose one's balance
intense, very strong
chest, large wooden or metal box
bolt, a bar to fasten a door or a lid
gaze, to look (at something) in surprise

knees, and, burying his naked arms in gold, let them remain there, as if enjoying the luxury of a bath. At length, with a deep sigh, he exclaimed,

"And dis all come of de goole-bug! de poor little goole-bug!"

It was growing late, and we had to get everything housed before daylight. It was difficult to say what should be done; and much time was spent discussing how the treasure could be removed. We finally lightened the box by removing two thirds of its contents. We were then able, with some trouble, to raise it from the hole. The articles taken out were hidden among the brambles, and the dog left to guard them. We then hurried homewards with the chest, reaching the hut, in safety, at one o'clock in the morning. It had been very hard work, and worn out as we were, we could do no more just then. We rested until two, had something to eat, and started for the hills immediately afterwards, armed with three large sacks.

A little before four we arrived at the hole. We divided the treasure, as equally as might be, among us and again set out for the hut where we arrived just as the first rays of early morning sun shone through the treetops in the East.

We were now completely broken down. We slept for some three or four hours and woke up to make an examination of our treasure.

The chest had been full, and we spent the whole day, and the greater part of the next night, going through its contents. Having sorted all with care, we found that we possessed an even greater wealth than we had first supposed. In coins there was rather more than four hundred and fifty thousand dollars. All was gold of very old date. There was French, Spanish, and German money, with a few English *guineas*. There were several very large and heavy coins, very old and worn. There was no American money. The value of the jewels was difficult to guess. There were diamonds – some of them extremely large and fine, a hundred and ten in all, and not one of them small; eighteen *rubies*, three hundred and ten *emeralds*, all very beautiful. Besides all this, there were nearly two hundred finger and ear rings; rich chains, thirty of these, if I remember; eighty-three very large and heavy *crucifixes*; one hundred and ninety-seven gold watches, all richly jewelled and in cases of great worth; all of this at least one milion and a half dollar worth.

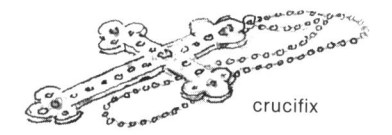

crucifix

When, at length, we had concluded our examination, Legrand, who saw how eager I was to hear the solution of this most extraordinary *riddle*, decided that it was the right moment to tell me the full story in detail.

"You remember," he said, "the night when I handed you the rough sketch I had made of the scarabæus. You remember also, that I became quite angry with you for insisting that my drawing resembled a death's-

---

guinea, English gold coin
ruby, emerald, very precious stones
riddle, puzzle; a mysterious question that must be solved by clever thinking

head. The first time you said this I thought you were joking. But afterwards I remembered the peculiar spots on the back of the insect, and admitted to myself that there was some truth in your remark. However, I was not pleased with your judgement of my talent as an artist – and, therefore, when you handed me the *scrap* of *parchment*, I was about to throw it angrily into the fire."

"The scrap of paper, you mean, "I said.

"No; it looked very much like paper, and at first I thought it was; but when I began to draw on it, I discovered, at once, that it was a piece of very thin parchment. It was quite dirty, you remember. Well, in the very act of throwing it into the fire, my glance fell upon the sketch at which you had been looking. You may imagine my surprise when I saw, in fact, the figure of a death's-head just where, it seemed to me, I had made the drawing of the beetle. For a moment I was too much *amazed* to think clearly. I knew that my drawing was very different in detail from this – although they were somewhat alike. I took a candle, and seating myself at the other end of the room, began to examine the parchment closely. Upon turning it over, I saw my own sketch on the other side, just as I had made it. What a strange *coincidence*, I thought, that unknown to me, there should have been a skull on the other side of the parchment, and that this, not only in outline, but in size, should so closely resemble my

---

scrap, a (small) piece; a slip
parchment, skin of a sheep, goat etc. prepared for writing
amazed, greatly surprised
coincidence, the occurring, by chance, at the same time or place of two or more events that appear to be connected

drawing. My mind struggled to make a connection – but was unable to do so. Then, gradually, I was able to think clearly again. I was now certain that there had been no drawing on the parchment when I made my sketch of the scarabæus. I became perfectly certain of this; for I remembered turning up first one side and then the other, in search for the cleanest spot. Had the skull been there, of course I could not have failed to notice it. Here was indeed a mystery which I felt it impossible to explain. I put the parchment safely away and put the whole question out of my mind until I was alone.

"When you had gone, and when Jupiter was fast asleep, I began a more careful investigation of the affair. In the first place I considered the manner in which the parchment had come into my possession. The spot where we discovered the scarabæus was on the coast of the mainland, about a mile eastward of the island, and only a short distance above high water mark. When I took hold of it, it gave me a sharp bite, which made me drop it. Jupiter looked about him for a leaf, or something of that nature, by which to take hold of it. His eye, and mine also, fell upon the scrap of parchment, which I then supposed to be paper. It was lying half buried in the sand, a corner sticking up. Near the spot where we found it, I observed what was left of a *hull*. The *wreck* seemed to have been there for a very great while.

"Well, Jupiter picked up the parchment, wrapped the beetle in it, and gave it to me. Soon afterwards we

---

hull, the frame or body of a ship
wreck, a greatly damaged ship

turned to go home, and on the way we met my friend from Fort Moultrie. I showed him the insect, and he begged me to let him take it to the fort, he is very interested in all subjects connected with Natural History. So I let him have it, and he put it in his pocket without the parchment which I had continued to hold in my hand while he was looking at the insect. Without thinking about it, I must have put it in my own pocket.

"You remember that I found no paper on my table, nor in the drawers when I wanted to draw a sketch of the beetle. I searched my pockets, hoping to find an old letter and then my hand fell upon the parchment.

"No doubt you will think me *fanciful* – but I already had made some kind of connection. I had put together two *links* of a great chain. There was a boat lying on a sea-coast, and not far from the boat was a parchment – not a paper – with a skull drawn on it. You will, of course, ask 'where is the connection?' I reply that the skull, or death's-head, is the well-known sign of the *pirate*. It is on the flag of the pirate's ship."

"But," I interrupted, "you say that the skull was not on the parchment when you made the drawing of the beetle. How then do you find any connection between the boat and the skull – since this latter, according to your own account, must have been drawn at some period after your sketching the scarabæus?"

"Ah, hereupon turns the whole mystery; although I had only little difficulty in solving the secret at this point. My steps were sure, and could arrive at only one

---

fanciful, having strange and unreal ideas
link, ring of a chain
pirate, a person who attacks and robs ships at sea

result. I reasoned thus: When I drew the scarabæus, no skull could be seen on the parchment. When I had completed the drawing, I gave it to you, and observed you closely until you returned it. You, therefore, did not draw the skull, and no one else was present to do it. Then it was not done by any human being. And nevertheless it was done.

"At this stage of my reflections I tried to remember, and did remember clearly, every event which occurred about the period in question. The weather was rather cold (oh rare and happy accident!), and a fire was burning. I was hot with exercise and sat near the table. You, however, had drawn a chair close to the fire. Just as I placed the parchment in your hand, and as you were about to look at it, Wolf, the Newfoundland, entered, and leaped upon your shoulders. You kept him off with your left hand, while your right, holding the parchment, was close to the fire. At one moment I thought it would catch fire, and was about to warn you, but, before I could speak, you had pulled your hand up and were engaged in examining the parchment. When I considered all these particulars, I doubted not for a moment that the heat had brought the skull to light on the parchment.

"You know, of course, that chemical preparations exist, and have existed time out of mind, by means of which it is possible to write so that the characters shall become *visible* only subjected to the action of fire. These colours disappear when the material written on cools, but again become visible when heated up again.

---

visible, able to be seen

"I now examined the death's-head with care. Parts of the drawing were clearer than others. The effect of the fire had not been complete. I immediately lit a fire, and subjected every part of the parchment to a strong heat. After a while, there became visible, at the corner of the slip opposite the death's-head, the figure of what I at first supposed to be a goat. I examined it carefully and became certain that it was meant to be a *kid*."

"Ha! Ha!" I said, "to be sure I have no right to laugh at a million and a half of money, but you are not about to make a third link in your chain – you will not find any special connection between your pirates and a goat! Pirates have no farming interests."

"But I have just said that the figure was not that of a goat;" said Legrand, "kid is not the same thing. You may have heard of Captain Kidd*. I at once looked at the figure of the animal as a kind of *signature*, as its position on the parchment suggested this idea. The death's-head at the corner opposite, had, in the same manner, the appearance of a stamp. But I was deeply disappointed not to find anything between the two."

"I suppose you expected to find a letter between the stamp and the signature."

"Something of that kind. The fact is, I had a very strong feeling that some good fortune was about to happen. I can hardly say why. Perhaps, after all, it was

---

kid, young goat
*Scottish sailor, fought for England against France off the North American coast. Commanded his own ship. Accused of being a pirate and hanged in England in 1701.
signature, a signed name

rather a desire than an actual belief. But Jupiter's silly words about the bug being of solid gold, had a powerful effect on my imagination. And then the series of accidents and coincidences. These were so very extraordinary. By accident all these events should occur on the only day of all the year in which it had been cool enough for a fire; and without a fire, or without the dog leaping upon you in the precise moment in which he appeared, I should never have noticed the death's-head, and so never come to possess the treasure."

"But go on – I can't wait to hear the rest!"

"Well; you have heard, of course, the many stories about money buried, somewhere on the Atlantic coast, by Kidd and his men. There must be some truth in these stories. They still exist, so it appeared to me that the treasure might still be buried. Had Kidd hidden his treasure for a time and then come back to take it with him again, these stories would hardly have reached us in their present unchanged form. You will observe that the stories told are all about money-seekers, not about money-finders. Had the pirate recovered his money, the affair would have ended there. It seemed to me that some accident had prevented him from coming back to get his money, and that this accident had become known to his followers. They came looking for the hidden treasure, but all in vain as they had no map or other means of finding it. And thus began the reports that are now so common.

"So Kidd's treasure was still buried somewhere near the coast, and I was certain that the parchment contained the solution to the mystery. It was very dirty, as you remember, and I thought it possible that the dirt

75

prevented the heat from having its effect. So I carefully poured warm water over it to clean it and, having done this, I placed it in a tin *pan*, with the skull downwards, and heated it up over the fire. In a few minutes, I removed the slip from the hot pan, and to my joy, found it spotted, in several places, with what appeared to be figures arranged in lines. Again I placed it in the pan for another minute. On taking it off, the whole was just as you see it now."

Here Legrand, having re-heated the parchment, handed it over to me. The following characters were now visible in red colour, between the death's-head and the goat:

53‡‡†305))6*;4826)4‡.)4‡);806*;48†8¶60))85;;]8*;:
‡*8†83(88)5*†;46(;88*96*?;8)*‡(;485);5*†2:*‡
(;4956*2(5*–4)8]8*;4069285);)6†8)4‡‡;1(‡9;48081;8:8
‡1;48†85;4)485†528806*81(‡9;48;(88;4(‡?34;48)
4‡;161;:188;‡?;

"But," I said, returning the slip, "I'm as much in the dark as ever. Were all the jewels in the world awaiting me on my solution of this riddle, I am quite sure that I should be unable to earn them."

"And yet," said Legrand, "the solution is by no means difficult. These characters, as one might readily guess, form a *cipher* – that is to say, they carry a meaning. I take an interest in riddles and have solved many far more difficult than this one, made up by the simple mind of a sailor.

---

pan, a metal pot used for cooking food
cipher, manner of secret writing

"The first question regards the language of the cipher. But, with the cipher now before us, all difficulty is removed by the signature. The picture of the goat reading Kidd is only possible in English.

"You observe there are no divisions between the words. Had there been, the task would have been quite easy. In such case I should have begun with an analysis of the shorter words, and, had a word of a single letter occurred, as is most likely (a or I, for example,) I should have solved it at once. But, there being no division, my first step was to find the most as well as the least frequent letter. Counting all, I made the following list:

Of the character 8 there are 33.
;	"	26.
4	"	19.
‡)	"	16.
*	"	13.
5	"	12.
6	"	11.
† 1	"	8.
0	"	6.
9 2	"	5.
: 3	"	4.
?	"	3.
]	"	2.
] –	"	1.

"Now, in English, the letter which most frequently occurs is e. Afterwards follow a o i d h n r s t u y c f g l m w b k p q x z. E however is so frequently used that there is rarely a sentence seen of any length where e does not appear several times.

"Here, then, we have, in the very beginning, the groundwork for something more than just a guess. As our most frequent character is 8, we will begin by *assuming* it as the e of the natural alphabet. Now, let us see if 8 is seen in couples – for e is frequently doubled in English – in such words as 'meet,' 'seen,' 'been,' 'agree,' etc. In the present instance we see it doubled no less than five times, although the message is short.

"Let us assume 8, then, as e. Now, of all words in the language 'the' is the most usual. Let us see, therefore, whether any three characters are repeated, in the same order, the last of them being 8. These three characters, so arranged, will most probably represent the word 'the.' Looking again, we find no less than seven such arrangements, the characters being ;48. We may, therefore, assume that ; represents t, that 4 represents h, and that 8 represents e – the last now being well confirmed. Thus a great step has been taken.

"Not only do we have the word 'the' but also the beginning and end of other words. For instance, the combination ;48 occurs not far from the end of the cipher. Of the six characters succeeding this 'the,' we already know five. Let us set these characters down by the letters we know them to represent, leaving a space for the unknown –

t eeth

"We can now immediately decide that the last th form no part of the word beginning with the first t. Going through the entire alphabet for a letter to put into the empty space, we find that no word can be

---

assume, to accept as true; to suppose

formed of which this th can be a part. We are thus narrowed into

t ee

and, going through the alphabet, if necessary, as before, we arrive at the word 'tree,' as the only possible reading. We thus gain another letter, r, represented by (, and can read 'the tree.'

"Looking beyond these words, for a short distance, we again see the combination ;48. We thus have this arrangement:

the tree ;4(‡?34the

"Let us now set down the characters with the letters we know, it reads thus:

the tree thr‡?3hthe

"Now let us write it in this way:

the tree th....h the

and the word 'through' makes itself clear at once. This discovery gives us three new letters, o, u, and g, represented by ‡? and 3.

"Looking now, narrowly, through the cipher for combinations of known characters, we find, not very far from the beginning this arrangement:

83)88, or egree,

which will form the word 'degree,' and gives us another letter, d, represented by †.

"Four letters beyond the word 'degree,' we find the combination,

;46(;88*

"Translating the known characters, and representing the unknown by *dots*, as before, we read thus:

th.rtee.

---

dot, a small, round mark

which immediately suggests the word "thirteen" and gives us two new letters, i and n, represented by 6 and *.

"In the beginning of the message, we find the combination

53‡‡†

"Translating, as before, we get

.good,

which assures us that the first letter is A, and that the first two words are 'A good.'

"It is now time that we arrange our key, as far as discovered. It will stand thus:

5	represents	a
†	–	d
8	–	e
3	–	g
4	–	h
6	–	i
*	–	n
‡	–	o
(	–	r
;	–	t

"We have, therefore, no less than ten of the most important letters represented, and it will not be necessary to go on with the details of the solution. It now only remains to give you the full translation of the characters on the parchment. Here it is:

"'A good glass in the *bishop's hostel* in the devil's seat

---

bishop, title within the Christian church of a person in charge of a group of churches; here the name of the *hostel*
hostel, inn

twenty-one degrees and thirteen minutes northeast and by north main branch seventh limb east side shoot from the left eye of the death's-head a bee-line from the tree through the shot fifty feet out.'"

"But," I said, "the riddle seems still in as bad a condition as ever. How is it possible to get any meaning from this nonsense about 'devil's seat,' 'death's-head,' and 'bishop's hostel'?"

"Yes, I know that it looks difficult at a first glance there being no division between the sentences. But I noticed that each time there would be a break in the subject where there would naturally be a pause or a point, he would run the characters, at this place, more than usually close together. Acting on this, I made the division thus:

"'A good glass in the Bishop's hostel in the Devil's seat twenty-one degrees and thirteen minutes northeast and by north – main branch seventh limb east side shoot from the left eye of the death's-head – a bee-line from the tree through the shot fifty feet out.'"

"Even this division," said I, "leaves me still in the dark."

"It left me also in the dark," replied Legrand, "for a few days, during which I made a careful inquiry, in the neighbourhood of Sullivan's Island, for any building which went by the name of the 'Bishop's Inn'; for, of course, I dropped the old word 'hostel.'

"One morning it entered into my head, quite suddenly, that this 'Bishop's Hostel' might have some reference to an old family, of the name of Bessop, which, time out of mind, had held possession of a large house, about four miles to the northward of the Island. I accordingly went there and inquired among the older negroes of the place. At length one of the most aged of the women said that she had heard of such a place as Bessop's Castle, and thought that she could guide me to it, but that it was not a castle, nor an inn, but a high rock.

"I offered to pay her well for her trouble, and she agreed to accompany me to the spot. We found it without much difficulty, and after she had left, I examined the place. The 'castle' was a mass of cliffs and rocks – one of the latter being very high and of an artificial appearance. I climbed to the top, and felt much at a loss as to what should be done next.

"My eyes then fell on a narrow *ledge* in the eastern face of the rock, perhaps a yard below the top on which I stood. This ledge was sticking out about eighteen inches, and was not more than a foot wide. The cliff above it was hollow and made it resemble a chair. I had no doubt that here was the 'devil's seat', and now I seemed to understand the full secret of the riddle.

"The 'good glass', I knew, could be nothing but a *telescope:* for the word 'glass' is often used in this sense by seamen. I hurried home, got a telescope, and returned to the rock.

"I let myself down to the ledge, and found that it was impossible to sit down on it unless in one particular position. This fact went well with the idea I had already formed in my mind. I now began to use the glass. Of course, the 'twenty-one degrees and thirteen minutes' could refer to nothing but the height above

---

ledge, a shelf or an object that sticks out like a shelf

telescope   compas

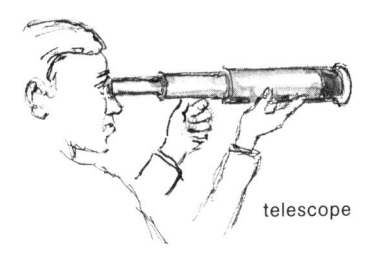

the horizon. The direction 'northeast and by north' I had found at once by means of a pocket-*compass*. Then, pointing the glass as best I could do it by guess, I moved it carefully up or down, until I stopped at a circular opening in the leaves of a large tree taller than the others. In the centre of this opening I could see a white spot, but could not, at first, distinguish what it was. I corrected the telescope in order to get a clear picture and looked again. I now made it out to be a human skull.

"I now considered the mystery solved. The phrase 'main branch, seventh limb, east side', could refer only to the position of the skull on the tree, while 'shoot from the left eye of death's-head' could only mean that one should drop a *bullet* from the left eye of the skull. A 'bee-line', or , in other words a straight line, drawn from the nearest point of the trunk through the 'shot', (or the spot where the bullet fell,) and then extended to a distance of fifty feet, would lead to the exact spot where the treasure was hidden."

"All this," I said, "is quite clear. When you left the Bishop's Hostel, what then?"

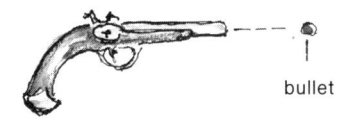

bullet

83

"Why, having carefully taken the *bearings* of the tree, I turned homewards. The instant that I left the 'devil's seat', however, the opening in the leaves disappeared, and I never saw it again, turn as I would. This opening is visible from no other point of view than that afforded by the narrow ledge on the face of the rock.

"On the next day I got up very early and went into the hills in search of the tree. I found it after much hard work. With the rest of the adventure I believe you are as well acquainted as myself."

"I suppose," I said, "you missed the spot, in the first attempt at digging, because Jupiter let the bug fall through the right instead of the left eye of the skull."

"Exactly. This mistake made a difference of about two inches and a half in the 'shot' that is to say, in the position of the peg nearest the tree; and had the treasure been beneath the 'shot', – the error would have been of little importance, but by the time we had gone fifty feet, we were far away from the hiding place."

"Why did you insist on letting fall the bug," I asked, "instead of a bullet, from the skull? I was sure you were quite mad."

"Why, to be honest, I felt a little angry that you believed me mad. So I decided to punish you quietly, in my own way, by a little *mystification*. For this reason I swung the beetle, and for this reason I let it fall from the tree. An observation of yours about its great weight suggested the latter idea."

"Yes, I see. And now there is only one point which

---

bearings, direction or relative position
mystification, something difficult to understand

puzzles me. What are we to make of the bones of the dead men found in the hole?"

"That is a question I am no more able to answer than yourself. There seems, however, only one way of accounting for them. It is clear that Kidd must have had help to bury the treasure. But when the hardest work was over, he may have thought it wisest to remove those who knew his secret – who shall tell?«

Questions

The Murders in the Rue Morgue

1. How do the writer and Dupin get acquainted?
2. What is interesting about Dupin in the writer's opinion?
3. What is unusual about the way they spend their time together?
4. How do the murders in the Rue Morgue come to their attention?
5. Describe the lives of the murdered women.
6. What do the neighbours and the gendarme find when they enter the house?
7. In what state are the corpses of the two women when finally discovered?
8. What is particular about the evidence given by neighbours and passers-by?
9. Give an account of the various problems that make this a difficult crime for the police to solve.
10. What reasons does Dupin have for taking an interest in the case?
11. How does he prove that it is possible to enter and leave the locked room? Describe his method of analysis.
12. What are the striking characteristics of the crime?
13. Which conclusion must these facts necessarily lead to?

14. Which other clues support this conclusion?
15. How does Dupin's analysis of all the facts lead him to the conclusion of the case?

The Gold-Bug

1. In which way is the fate of Legrand similar to that of Dupin?
2. What is particular about the beetle found by Legrand?
3. What happens when he wants to describe it to his friend, the writer?
4. What does Jupiter tell the writer when he brings him his master's message?
5. Describe the expedition to the tulip-tree.
6. What is the purpose of the death's-head?
7. What does the chest contain?
8. Describe Legrand's way of reasoning when he had seen the death's-head on the parchment.
9. How does he bring the secret message to light?
10. Which problems arise after the secret message has been spelled out in normal letters?
11. How does Legrand solve the riddle?
12. Why didn't Legrand tell his friend the meaning of the secret message at once?
13. Make a list of sentences that would be different in modern English.